The Secrets of Magnolia Moon

With love and gratitude
to Nancy Conescu and Alex Wyatt

This is a work of fiction. Names, characters, places and incidents are either the product of the author's imagination or, if real, are used fictitiously. All statements, activities, stunts, descriptions, information and material of any other kind contained herein are included for entertainment purposes only and should not be relied on for accuracy or replicated as they may result in injury.

First published in Great Britain 2020 by Walker Books Ltd
87 Vauxhall Walk, London SE11 5HJ

2 4 6 8 10 9 7 5 3 1

This book has been typeset in Veronan

Printed and bound in Germany

British Library Cataloguing in Publication Data:
a catalogue record for this book is available
from the British Library

ISBN 978-1-4063-9349-1

www.walker.co.uk

The Secrets of Magnolia Moon

EDWINA WYATT

illustrated by KATHERINE QUINN

WALKER BOOKS

For Henry and Audrey

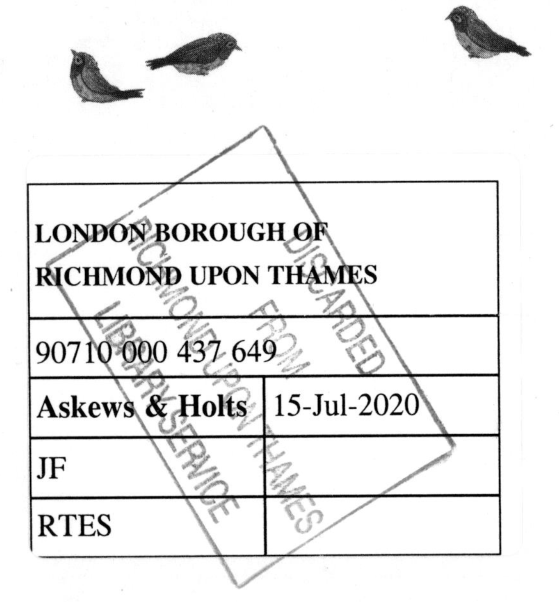

Chapter 1:

The Secret Goodbye

Magnolia Moon was born on a hill in a very great hurry. It was the moon that kissed her first. It put the dimple in her cheek and the coils in her hair. But that is a secret. Her mother is sure they come from her.

The moon and the girl have been friends ever since. They have much in common. There is her surname, of course, which she can spell backwards as well as forwards. Her size, too, because she looks small from the window (but it's only a trick). For although she has spent many of her nine years reaching on tiptoes, her socks always slipping down, her heart is two sizes bigger than most. She makes other things bigger too, as jelly snakes and Sunday afternoons all stretch further when she invites you to dance the Heel and Toe Polka through the sloping streets of Thistledown. *Heel and toe. Heel and toe. Slide. Slide. Slide. Slide.* Clapping both hands and a few times on the knees before pausing for a drink at the fountain.

And much like the moon, Magnolia likes hiding. Behind her book of Greek myths, or a dark cloud of hair filled with small, precious things. Feathers. Twigs. A secret or two. Magnolia Moon is very good at keeping secrets. She knows just what to do with them, and has a way of talking to the jumpy ones to stop them causing trouble. Which is why people are always leaning in and whispering:

"Can I tell you a secret?"

"If you like," she shrugs and peers at you through her beetle-black curls.

Which is how it happened just now.

"I'm leaving," said Imogen May.

"Oh?" said Magnolia, dropping the leaf she was twirling.

They were sitting beneath the Wishing Tree in Imogen May's back garden, when the summer breeze felt suddenly cool.

"Mum got a new job somewhere else."

"Oh," said Magnolia again, losing the ant she was following. "When do you leave?"

"Tomorrow morning."

"Tomorrow!" said Magnolia. "We're about to start Year Four! There's a whole year to go, which is a lifetime if you are a giant jellyfish."

Imogen May agreed. A year was a very long time.

"Where are you going?"

"To Barrow."

Magnolia gasped, both socks slipping down in disappointment. "Barrow is a whole hour away, which is a lifetime if you are a cake in the oven!"

Imogen May nodded sadly. An hour was a very long time.

"Are you really going?" said Magnolia, trying not to be cross.

"Yes," said Imogen May, peeling off a patch of moss. "But don't tell anyone. I don't like saying goodbye."

The two friends sat beneath the Wishing Tree in silence, Magnolia wondering gloomily if they would ever again hang upside-down from the old fig, inventing new kinds of animals or guessing what type of fruit they would be. Imogen May Bell had always lived just around the corner – so close that Magnolia could hear the wind chimes tinkling on the Bell family's verandah at night. There would be farms and fences and rivers between them now. However, Magnolia tugged up her socks, since it was not yet tomorrow and Imogen May was still here. She climbed onto the tree and got thinking.

"I would be a grape," said Magnolia, swinging upside-down.

"Why?" said Imogen May, finding a branch and swinging beside her.

"Because you would never be lonely, sitting there in a bunch. You would always have someone to talk to."

"What if you rolled off and went under the table? Grapes always get squashed."

"I hadn't thought of that. Can I change my answer?"

"No, you cannot," said Imogen May. "Purple or green?"

"Purple," said Magnolia. "Or are they called red grapes?"

Imogen May pondered this for a moment.

"I would be a grapefruit," she said.

"Why?"

"Because nobody wants a grapefruit. Too sour. So nobody would take you away from your home in the fruit bowl. You could stay with your friends forever and ever."

"What about the peliphants?" said Magnolia.

"What are *they*?"

"Half pelican. Half elephant. And they only eat grapefruit."

Imogen May grimaced. "Do they have a bill or a trunk?"

"A trunk. And they only want the *skin* of the grapefruit."

"Oh," said Imogen May, wrinkling her nose. "May I change my answer?"

"No," said Magnolia. "You may not."

Then they looked around and saw the sun was setting, the day suddenly done.

When it was time to say goodbye, Magnolia opened her mouth before shutting it promptly again. Then she raised her arm before dropping it swiftly, unsure of what to do, since Imogen May did not like goodbyes. Instead, she nodded once and turned sharply on her heels, her feet as muddled as her head.

On the corner of Chimneypot Parade, Magnolia turned around. Imogen May had already gone. The street was quiet. *Too* quiet. She ran home to 84 Crocus Cottage, where it was never quiet, what with Mama Moon teaching the piano all day, Daddy Moon learning the oboe and a crotchety staircase that barked whenever you trod too hard upon its back.

When Magnolia came through the front door, there was a honk and a horrible croak, as though a goose had swallowed a toad by accident. But it was only her father trying to play a duet with one of her mother's students, Eleanor Mink.

"From the top?" called Daddy Moon.

"I'll count you in," replied Mama Moon from her stool beside Eleanor, who was looking rather pale.

Atlas, the family cat, flattened his ears and followed Magnolia into the kitchen.

After dinner, Magnolia went upstairs and flopped on her bed. She could hear the wind chimes at Imogen May's. She traced a finger across the wall, making loops and curls.

N follows O, follows O, follows M. Magnolia liked writing her name backwards. It helped her think.

She wrote it in the flour on the kitchen bench. She wrote it in the sky on her way to school. She liked the way it sounded out loud, like an ancient language:

NOOM AILONGAM

Magnolia turned her pillow to the cool side, trying not to scratch the mosquito bite on her chin. She wondered how Imogen May was feeling. Pictured her cross-legged on the floor, packing her books and clothes into boxes to be loaded onto the truck tomorrow. Was she excited? Scared? Magnolia wanted to ask. She wanted to say goodbye. But Imogen May didn't like saying goodbye.

Sitting in the dark, Magnolia felt a sudden prickle of loneliness. Except she was not alone. A visitor was waiting at the window. Magnolia opened the curtains, peering up at the familiar face.

Hello.

Hello, blinked the moon.

Magnolia giggled as the moon painted her walls with its silvery brush. It made her pyjamas all patchy like the coat of a giraffe. She felt her bed begin to rise, imagining she was the goddess Artemis from her book of Greek myths, driving her moon chariot across the heavens. Then she remembered her troubles and sank back to the ground with a thump. The secret was hot in her mouth and flew out in a whispery rush.

"Imogen May is leaving tomorrow!"

The moon grew pale, a small chip crumbling off.

"She doesn't like saying goodbye, so nobody will know."

The moon rocked in the wind, deep in thought.

Then another face appeared at the window. Magnolia lifted the corner of her quilt and gave it a little shake. Atlas padded across her mattress, purring his thick honey-drizzle purr.

Magnolia yawned. She had said goodbye to so many things. Her pet ladybird. Her grandfather. The heart-shaped pearl in her favourite ring that fell out on her way to the shops. The handle on her watering can. And she said goodbye to the moon every morning when the sun came up. It didn't matter that there was a day and a world between them – they were still friends, even from a distance. Maybe that was how it would be with Imogen May. They could already communicate from a distance; had been sending secret notes for years. Across the room. Across the playground. With just a look or a twitch, Imogen May knew what Magnolia was trying to say, even when she said nothing at all. Even when the words came out wrong, all jumbled up and backwards like her name on the wall.

Then Magnolia's toes tingled. Her eyes glowed. What about a *secret* goodbye?

The next morning, Magnolia tried sneaking down the stairs, except her footsteps woke them up.

"*Move it!*" coughed the top stair.

"*Shh!*" wheezed the ones at the bottom.

Magnolia jumped and hit her head on the wooden ceiling beam. A bump was already forming.

"Shush, yourself!" she snapped back. "Stop being horrible."

But she regretted it immediately. The stairs had been sick with a summer cold, the hall being so full of draughts. A cold was guaranteed to make anyone grouchy.

She took down the craft box from the laundry cupboard. Inside she found some paste, cardboard and some leftover crepe paper from the iceberg she had made for her Year Three art project. Then she found some scissors and her best coloured pens that she had got for her birthday last Saturday, and spread it all out on the kitchen table.

"What's all this?" said Daddy Moon as he packed his bag.

"It's a secret," said Magnolia, making pink and gold streaks.

Once she was finished, Magnolia took her work out into the street, leaving a trail of glitter down the garden path. Atlas and her parents followed her curiously around the corner until they heard the *ting* of the wind chimes outside Imogen May's house.

As they came down Chimneypot Parade, Magnolia saw Mrs Bell on the stairs with a box labelled KITCHEN and Mr Bell in the garage with another marked FRAGILE. They were so busy that they didn't notice the small crowd that was standing on the street. There was a yelp and a gurgle as Imogen May's baby brother, Felix, was strapped into his car seat beside her other brother, Ernest. Magnolia was fond of Ernest, although he always seemed afraid of her. It couldn't be easy being four. Then Magnolia saw Imogen May. She was walking around the side of her house, touching the leaves of the thick wisteria vine that trailed the front verandah. She plucked off a leaf before opening the car door and sitting inside, lost in the sea of pot plants, jackets and pillows that were stuffed in the back seat. Her eyes were red and puffy. Before Magnolia could call out, the other doors slammed and the engine rumbled. She saw Felix flapping his arms wildly through the window.

As the car rolled down the driveway, Magnolia held the yellow cardboard sign above her head and chanted the words printed in thick purple letters:

"YAM NEGOMI EYBDOOG!"

At first the words felt rough and scratchy, but after she had said them a few more times, they rolled off her tongue in soft, round shapes. Then Mama Moon and Daddy Moon began bouncing on their toes too, and calling:

"YAM NEGOMI EYBDOOG!"
"YAM NEGOMI EYBDOOG!"

It wasn't long before the Minks and the Snows and the Lawsons and Polly Eggers and everybody from Chimneypot Parade stopped squinting through their windows and came out in their dressing gowns and slippers. Even Casper Sloan, the new boy who didn't say very much, had come outside with his droopy-eared dog. After looking to the left and the right and then back to the left again, they clapped their hands and stomped their feet, chanting: "YAM NEGOMI EYBDOOG", adding in extra bits for all the other Bells, until the words made a ribbon around them, drawing them together and leading the way down the road.

The car paused in the street with the windows down and while Imogen May's eyes were still red and puffy, she was laughing for joy, her hands full of all the kisses she had caught.

Magnolia watched the car make its way around the corner, nodding as Imogen May promised to look out for a brand-new Wishing Tree for them by the time she came to visit.

And though there were yells and hollers and whoops, not one person said goodbye.

For Magnolia Moon was very good at keeping secrets.

Dad's Stuff
FRAGILE
37ALF

Chapter 2:

The Secret Envelope

Magnolia Moon checked her watch. *Still early.* It was only three minutes since she had last checked, but that was a lifetime if you were a piece of toast or a soft-poached egg.

Magnolia didn't like being early. There was no one to talk to in the queue outside the classroom. For years, Imogen May had been the first to arrive at Thistledown Preparatory. Not any more, now that she went to a different school.

The new boy, Casper Sloan, was early too. Casper didn't want to talk. Not when Magnolia walked past his house. Not when she saw him at the shops or in the waiting room at the doctor's office. He seemed pleased to be left alone. Magnolia pulled up her socks. She stooped to tie and untie her shoelaces. Casper zipped and unzipped his bag, fumbling around inside. *Good idea,* thought Magnolia, zipping and unzipping her own bag, pretending to search for something deep down.

When her new teacher, Mr Hawkins, arrived, she followed him inside.

"Find a hook," he said. "Anywhere you like."

Magnolia went to the wall and hung up her school bag. She stared at the empty hook beside it, where Imogen May's bag would have gone. The other students rushed through the door and started jostling at the wall. Casper Sloan hurried past them and went straight to his desk, tucking his bag beneath his feet.

Finding her place, Magnolia watched Mr Hawkins hovering between the desks like a hummingbird. She liked him already. He had twinkly eyes and rode a green bicycle. Still without Imogen May, Year Four would be like a plum pudding without custard, or a pond without frogs.

On Magnolia's desk were an envelope and a strip of paper. When Mr Hawkins had finished handing out the rest, he told everybody to write down three things they would like to achieve this year.

"At the end of the year, I will give you back your envelope," said Mr Hawkins. "If you reached your goals, great! If you didn't, that's OK too. It's important to reflect on how things have changed."

"What's a goal?" asked Peggy Small.

"Think of it like a plan," said Mr Hawkins. "Something you would like to happen in the future."

"Like a wish?" asked Wren Snow.

"A bit like a wish," said Mr Hawkins. "But something that you can work hard to make happen on your own. It can be little or big. There is no wrong answer."

"I want to ride a cow!" said Adrian March.

"Well..." said Mr Hawkins, seeming to regret his last statement. "Write it down."

He zig-zagged between the desks, handing out extra pencils.

"And no talking with your neighbour," he said, his smiley eyes twinkling. "This is just for you."

Magnolia glanced around. Everybody had their heads down and their arms curled around their secret hopes. Everybody except Casper Sloan. He was looking out the window at a crow pecking rubbish. It hopped from side to side in a strange little jig, warbling merrily.

Crow, thought Magnolia. *I want to learn how to speak Crow. Just like Grandma Moon.* A small smile crossed her face as she pictured her grandmother cawing from her verandah in her cowboy boots. She wrote down:

SPEAK CROW

And marked it with an underline.

Then Magnolia sharpened her pencil and began work on her second goal. She knew just what she wanted to do:

FLY WITH THE ANGEL

Staring down at the words, she could already feel the sting of the wind on her face as she drifted over spires and treetops. She remembered the first time she saw the angel. She had been waiting outside the town hall, dropping coins into the wishing well, when a long shadow fell across the cobblestones. A grand, winged creature was perched on the wall behind her. She thought that her wish had come true – that one of the angels carved into the stone around the old astral clock had come to life. Then she saw that it wasn't an angel. It was a boy. Tall and willowy. His arms outstretched like vast, pale wings. His bare feet poised like a dancer's. She watched him crouch and draw himself in, as though being pulled tight by an invisible archer. Then he shot from the wall and soared past her, his long hair streaming behind him like torn cobwebs. She had never seen anyone run so fast.

Peggy Small and her friends had pointed and giggled as they watched him glide through the town square. Yet the angel boy didn't look back to see where the laughter came from. He didn't seem to care. He was somewhere else, high above, flying through his own secret sky.

"Who was that?" Magnolia had asked Peggy Small, when he had disappeared down a shadowy lane.

"I don't know," she had said and laughed again. She was still laughing now, across the room with her friends. Magnolia looked to the wall and saw their matching bags hanging beside each other in a row. The hook beside her bag was still empty. Imogen May was still not here. And there was still nobody to talk to. Starting a new line, she wrote down one more thing, folded the paper in half and sealed up the envelope.

Glancing around to see who else had finished, her eyes landed on Casper Sloan. He was twiddling his pencil and tapping out a beat on the desk. She had seen him patting his dog in his front garden sometimes. It was an old dog with floppy lips and sad eyes, and she wished that she could pat it too. Casper stopped tapping and scratched his nose. Magnolia tried not to look at what he had written on his piece of paper – although she couldn't help wondering what someone like Casper might secretly hope for. She turned away and decorated her envelope with squiggly lines.

"One more minute," said Mr Hawkins. Paper rustled and there were whispers as everyone rushed to finish. Then Casper began folding up his sheet. Magnolia closed her eyes, but her right eye got away from her. And before she could shut it again, she saw what was written on her neighbour's paper as he slipped it into its envelope. Nothing. Not a single word. Casper Sloan's paper was blank.

As Mr Hawkins walked past to collect the envelopes, the classroom erupted in a burst of chatter.

Casper glanced at Magnolia. She could tell that *he* knew what *she* knew.

They stared at each other for a moment. Magnolia felt a little red kite of hope dive and swoop inside. Casper opened his mouth to say something, then bowed his head, unzipped his bag and began rooting around inside again.

Magnolia seized her chance.

"If you could be a fruit, any fruit, what would you be?"

"Sorry?" said Casper.

"If you could be a fruit, any fruit—"

"Yes, I did hear you; I'm just not sure what you mean. How can you *be* a fruit and why would you want to be?"

Magnolia sighed. The little red kite crashed inside her, and she ached all over again for Imogen May, who would never ask such a question. Instead she would say: "I would be a watermelon."

"Why?" Magnolia would answer.

"Because they are always tricking people. On the outside they are green and hard. But on the inside, they are pink and squishy."

"What about all those seeds?" Magnolia would ask. "You would always be getting picked at."

And because Imogen May wouldn't like to be picked at – told to tidy up and brush her hair – she would ask if she could change her answer to a *seedless* watermelon. (Because she had seen them at Mr Silk's fruit shop, although she had never tried one since her mother said they were too expensive.)

And Magnolia Moon would refuse.

Yet Casper was not Imogen May. Casper was Casper. Perhaps it wasn't fair to compare apples with oranges, and she should stay away from fruit altogether. Magnolia thought of something else to ask.

"What's your dog's name?"

"Bonnie."

"She's lovely," said Magnolia.

"Excuse me," he said. "I've got to get something ... in here."

Casper thrust his head further into his schoolbag. Magnolia felt her sock begin to droop and she turned to the window.

The crow outside pecked at a paper bag.

After school, Casper was walking down the hill. Magnolia ran to catch him up. She couldn't keep it inside any longer.

"Couldn't you think of anything?"

Casper didn't look surprised. This time, he knew just what she was talking about.

"I could," he said, staring at his feet. "I know exactly what I want."

"Then why didn't you write it down?"

"Because those things will never happen," said Casper. "So I'm saving myself the trouble of hoping."

Magnolia understood.

It hurt to be disappointed. But Grandpa Moon used to say that there was always hope. That the seeds of hope can live in the darkest places – in the deepest holes and cracks of a broken heart. Fed by tears. Fuelled by courage. Wending their way towards the light until they bloomed inside. Growing into something new and unexpected. Instead of telling Casper this, she snapped her jelly snake in two and gave him the big bit. Still, she wondered what Casper hoped for as she waved goodbye.

As Magnolia walked home, she thought about all the things she had hoped for before. It was hope that made grass grow and waves rise and babies stand. And when the grass got trampled, the waves crashed down and babies toppled over, it was hope that made them stretch up all over again. And it was hope that made the angel boy fly, that made him believe that one day, his heels really might lift off the ground.

The next morning, Magnolia checked her watch. *Still early.* So was Casper.

"Hi," said Casper.

"Hello," said Magnolia.

Casper went to unzip his bag, then he put it down.

"Did you hear the wind last night?"

Magnolia nodded.

"I thought the roof was going to lift off!" she said.

Casper made a small pile of leaves with his foot.

"It was so noisy, I checked to see if the Anemoi were in the garden."

"Who are they?" asked Casper.

"They're the wind gods. I like Greek mythology. I have a book all about it. You can borrow it sometime, if you like?"

"I would, thank you. What are they like?"

"Well, it depends what direction they are coming from. Boreas is the north wind and so he is quite cold and frosty. Then there's Zephyrus, the west wind who is warmer and—"

"Good morning, Magnolia. Morning, Casper," said Mr Hawkins, walking past and unlocking the classroom. He was still wearing his bicycle helmet.

When Magnolia sat down at her desk, Casper's school bag was tucked under his seat.

"There's a spare hook over here," said Magnolia. "Beside mine."

Magnolia took Casper over to the wall and helped him hang up his bag.

"Can I tell you a secret?" whispered Casper, the tips of his ears going pink.

"If you like," said Magnolia, peering at him through her beetle-black hair.

"I know I didn't write anything down yesterday, but if I had, I think I could cross one of those things off today."

Magnolia's toes tingled. Her eyes glowed.

"Me too," she said.

The crow hopped past the classroom. It pecked at a peach stone and warbled loudly.

"What do you think it's saying?" said Magnolia.

Casper cocked his head to one side and listened. "It said *peaches are tasty, but I prefer nectarines.*"

Magnolia looked at Casper, her mouth forming a small "o".

"I can speak Crow, you know," said Casper. "Fox, too. Maybe I could teach you?"

Magnolia laughed, her springy hair bouncing.

That was *two* things she would be able to cross off her list in her secret envelope. A whole year early, too. Magnolia Moon decided that she did like being early, after all.

And somewhere, high in the clouds, a little red kite dived and swooped.

Chapter 3:

The Secret Song

Magnolia loved getting into her parents' bed. It fit all three of them perfectly. Each with their own place in the universe. Mama on the left, Daddy on the right and Magnolia in the middle. She loved the indigo sheets dotted with stars that looked like a grand old sky.

Magnolia swam across the stars to find her spot. Mama Moon was singing Magnolia's song. Her special song. The one about the little moon. It's how she got her favourite nickname: Little Moon.

Although they never used it when she was in trouble.

"Can we tell you a secret, Little Moon?" whispered Daddy.

"If you like," said Magnolia.

"There's going to be a New Moon in the sky. You're going to be a big sister."

Magnolia sat up. She liked babies, especially Felix, Imogen May's baby brother.

Round and rosy like a cherry tomato. Magnolia scrambled over the ring of pillows that she had made to get a closer look.

"Hellooooo," she called, putting her mouth against Mama Moon's belly.

No answer.

"You feel different," said Magnolia, shuffling to find the spot under Mama's arm that she usually fit into, like a jigsaw piece. She couldn't find it.

"A lot of things might feel different to start with," said Mama Moon.

"What like?"

"Well," said Mama Moon, glancing at Daddy

Moon, "at first things will be a little busier, noisier ... *messier.*"

Magnolia breathed a sigh of relief. Number 84 Crocus Cottage was the busiest, noisiest, messiest place she knew, so that was nothing to worry about.

"Also, a little squashier," said Mama Moon. "So you will have to share your room eventually."

Magnolia tried to suck the sigh right back in until her cheeks nearly popped.

"Like a sleepover every night," added Mama Moon quickly.

Magnolia relaxed and let it go. She loved sleepovers.

"What else?"

"Hard to say. Babies have a way of making their own plans. And babies love surprises."

Magnolia beamed. She loved surprises too.

"When will it come?"

"Only six months to go now," said Mama Moon.

"Six months!" howled Magnolia. "But that is a lifetime if you are a bedbug!"

"It's lucky that you're not a bedbug then," said Daddy Moon, beginning to itch at the thought. "Although it's time you went to bed. You have a big day tomorrow."

Back in her own room, Magnolia looked for a familiar face at the window. But the sky was a sea of clouds.

"Helloooo!" she called.

No answer.

Unable to find the moon, she called for Atlas.

"Hellooooo!"

No answer.

He would be out by now, on his evening walk.

Magnolia listened for the familiar *ting* of Imogen May's wind chimes. But there was no sound. They had taken them when they had moved to their new house. Everything was changing. And although she smiled in the dark at the thought of being a big sister, in a small, shadowy corner of her heart, a secret song began to play. Because Magnolia liked being the Little Moon of the family. She liked things just the way they were.

Magnolia woke early. A thought sprouted from her head like a bean shoot. *It's today!*

She rushed downstairs, being careful not to tread too hard on the old wooden staircase and wake it up – it was always stiff and grumpy in the morning.

"It's today!" she said to anyone who wanted to know. Although Atlas didn't. Daddy Moon was practising his oboe, and Mama Moon was in the shower.

But it didn't much matter. Since today she was going to drive all the way to Barrow to see Imogen May. Today she would see the new Wishing Tree that Imogen May had promised she would find, and they would hang upside-down, guessing what type of fruit they would be and making up new kinds of animals. Today it would be just like it had always been before Imogen May had moved. Magnolia hurried back upstairs to get dressed.

"Oomph!" grumbled the staircase, as she took two stairs at a time. *"Slow down."*

Mama Moon agreed, reminding her from the top that it was only three weeks since the girls had seen each other. Still, Magnolia didn't slow down, because that was a lifetime if you were a bar of soap.

The road to Barrow stretched for miles. They passed farms and fences and rivers.

It was a long drive, made longer by the fact that Mama Moon couldn't sit down for long. The baby growing inside made her back sore and her ankles swell. So Magnolia and Mama Moon stopped four times on the way, to stand and stretch on the side of the road. They picked clover and talked to the sheep and cows in neighbouring fields.

When Magnolia arrived, Imogen May came running through the grass.

Her house was tall and new. Not like her old cottage in Chimneypot Parade with the creaky verandah, covered with vines. There were no wind chimes or colourful pots. And it wasn't only the house that had changed. Imogen May also seemed different from how Magnolia remembered her. Although she couldn't work out how.

They squinted at each other through narrowed eyes. And as though she had read Magnolia's mind, Imogen May tilted her head to one side.

"You look different," she said.

"So do you."

But when they went inside, Magnolia smelled the familiar scent of the spices the Bells always cooked with. She recognized all their old furniture, the pictures on the wall, and, *ting!* Magnolia peered through the kitchen window and there they were, the old wind chimes, hanging from a pipe on the garden shed. Magnolia opened her mouth to speak, and Imogen May made a low hushing sound.

She took Magnolia by the hand and led her through the kitchen. There were piles of washing by the machine, spilling out of the basket in a tsunami of towels and sheets and tiny vests.

"Let's go outside," she whispered, stepping over a mound of socks and undies. "Felix is sleeping. *Again.*" Imogen May rolled her eyes. "He didn't sleep much last night and everyone is cross today. Even Ernest. They will be even crosser if I wake him up. They are always getting cross with me now."

That doesn't sound like much fun, Magnolia thought. Perhaps she didn't like babies after all. She didn't want her parents to be cross with her when their new baby arrived. She didn't like the way Mama's mouth went all thin and Daddy's eyebrows went all crooked when they were upset. Maybe this was what they meant when they said things would be different now. And it was happening already. Even *Imogen May* was different. A few notes of the secret song that Magnolia had been hearing wandered across her heart. The rhythm made her feet feel slow and her shoulders heavy.

Magnolia and Imogen May stood beneath the washing line and shuffled their feet.

"Can I tell you a secret?" said Imogen May.

"If you like," said Magnolia.

"I couldn't find us a new Wishing Tree."

"Oh," said Magnolia, a curl uncoiling in disappointment. "That's OK."

They glanced at each other shyly, unsure of what to do next.

"Do you want a drink?"

"Yes, please."

Imogen May went inside and wobbled back with a heavy tray. She poured Magnolia a glass of lemonade and passed her a plate of biscuits with pink and white icing.

"Guess what?" said Magnolia, taking a biscuit.

"You're going to fly around the world in a hot air balloon with a badger called Alphonse?"

"No," said Magnolia, deflating. "My mum is having a baby."

"Wow!" said Imogen May. "That's even better."

Magnolia wasn't convinced.

"Do you like it here?" she said, brushing the crumbs off her chest.

"It's OK. I miss you and I miss our Wishing Tree. But there are good things, too."

"What sort of things?"

"Well, there's a lizard that lives under the stairs, and a pile of old bricks, and a midnight train, and a big bush with magical red berries that you can use to make paint out of."

Magnolia brightened. Those *were* good things. She loved the rattly sound of trains too. And she had never tried making paint.

"Although the birds are always eating the berries and sitting on the washing line, leaving red stains on the clean sheets and we have to wash them all over again. Dad hisses at them and does this silly dance. But they don't care."

Magnolia looked up at the empty washing line. Then her toes tingled. Her eyes glowed.

"What are you doing?" called Imogen May as Magnolia dragged a pile of sheets out of the laundry. She pegged them to the washing line, draping them like a cloak of spring leaves across bare winter branches.

Then she dragged two milk crates along the cement and lay backwards upon one, the top of her head resting on the grass.

"It's a Washing Tree!" Magnolia grinned.

Imogen May grinned back and did the same. They dangled upside-down beneath the Washing Tree, staring at the patches of blue sky above. And soon enough, the birds joined in and warbled above them, their beaks stained red with crimson juice.

And as Magnolia Moon watched Imogen May hanging beside her, Imogen May looked just as she always did. Not a bit different. And it occurred to Magnolia that it was simply that she was so used to seeing her friend upside-down that it had been a shock to see her the right way up.

"I would be an avocado," said Imogen May.

"Why?" said Magnolia.

"Because you could live a double life as a fruit *and* a vegetable. Get to see things from the other side and report back – shake up the salad bowl. Like a secret salad agent."

"Is an avocado a fruit or a vegetable?"

"Exactly. It's a mystery."

Magnolia thought about this for a moment before taking her turn.

"I would be a mango."

"Big mistake," said Imogen May.

"Why?"

"Because that's what buffadillos eat."

"What are *they*?" asked Magnolia, her hair twisting into even springier coils with excitement since everything was back to normal.

"An armadillo crossed with a buffalo."

Magnolia nodded and said in that case she would be a honeydew melon. Although, of course, Magnolia already knew what a buffadillo was. There were two in her garden. Plus, a walramingo.

But that is a secret.

Chapter 4:
The Secret Escape

Magnolia Moon pressed her nose against the kitchen window and wiggled from side to side. She was trying to make Mama laugh. It was working. Florence Moon's cheeks were beginning to bloom and her eyes were lighting up. Yet no matter how much Magnolia wiggled, the dark rings around Mama's eyes would not budge.

Magnolia came inside and bowed very low.

"May I have this dance?" she said, slamming shut the recipe book that her mother was frowning over. It was Daddy Moon's turn to make dinner, but he was working late again.

"You may," Mama Moon curtseyed, fanning her face with a saucepan lid. "Mind my beans."

Florence Moon was a dreadful cook. Her face would turn very pink and there would be enough huffing and puffing coming from the kitchen to blow out a whole cake full of candles.

Out into the street they went, dancing the polka up the hill. *Heel and toe, heel and toe*, past shop windows and Casper Sloan's front door, *slide, slide, slide, slide*, over the bridge to the town square, clapping both hands and a few times on the knees before pausing for a drink at the fountain.

"Right!" gasped Magnolia, swinging her mother hard to the right.

"Left!" panted Mama Moon, swinging Magnolia hard to the left.

Back down the hill they went. *Heel and toe, heel and toe*, all the way. Leaping over ants. Kicking up leaves. Stopping only to wave to Casper. Then on they went, *slide, slide, slide, slide,* back to 84 Crocus Cottage. They were hard to miss, they laughed so wildly.

After dinner, Magnolia sat with Atlas by the window, listening very hard and "sharpening her senses" as Grandma Moon did. She longed for the crunch of gravel outside, her father's heavy footfalls coming up the garden path. But all she could hear was the secret song inside her, rising up from some shadowy place.

"Snowdrops!" her mother had cursed when she was spooning out the beans. And Magnolia had known then that Daddy Moon would not be home for dinner. It was their private code. Jeremy Moon was a bookkeeper. What he did precisely at his desk all day and night, Magnolia didn't know. She had several books on the shelf in her bedroom, and they didn't want very much keeping at all: only a bit of light dusting from time to time. What she did know was that her father was always tired, and that his work was never finished. He was forever dashing out the door, dropping kisses on heads. Which was why they had created their code word:

snowdrops. Since her father, too, burst forth in a flurry and then disappeared like a spring bloom. When Mama Moon was feeling especially irritated by her husband's comings and goings, she would declare her hatred of those fussy little flowers. Vow that she would never *dream* of planting snowdrops in the garden. Not even in the wild tangled jungle at the bottom that nobody ever visited.

"What's the point?" she'd say. "They just die off before you've had a chance to see them."

"Except they don't die," Daddy Moon would say. "They go back down to their roots and take the summer off." He promised that they would take the summer off too. Visit faraway places when the weather got warm. However, they never did. He was always too busy, too tired.

"Can I tell you a secret, Little Moon?" said Mama, plonking down beside Magnolia. Her fingers were cracked and sore from teaching piano all week.

"If you like," shrugged Magnolia, blowing her hair out of her eyes.

"It's Daddy's birthday on Saturday,"

Magnolia liked birthdays, although she would have to wait a while for hers. Magnolia counted on her fingers. *Wednesday. Thursday. Friday. Saturday.* Three days to prepare.

"Why is it a secret?"

"Because Daddy *thinks* it is. He rubbed it off the calendar."

"We should get him a present."

"That's the thing. He wants to keep it a secret since he doesn't want us to spend too much money. We're saving up."

"We have to get him *something*. Something he really needs."

Then Atlas's ears twitched. Mama's eyes widened. And Magnolia jumped up. Because they had all heard a crunch outside, the sound of heavy footfalls coming up the garden path.

As Magnolia emptied the rubbish into the bins beside the house, she saw her old friend hanging in the sky. The moon was almost full tonight, although its edges were smeared and faded. Beside it was the constellation Taurus – the bull made of stars. Grandma Moon had told her all about Cerus, the wild bull controlled by his emotions that would destroy fields of new flowers and frighten the villagers. Persephone, the spring goddess, had understood him, calmed him, even though the bull could not speak. The two had become great friends and she would ride on his back each spring. Together they would bring life to the blossoms. It was Grandma Moon that had given Magnolia the book of Greek myths for her last birthday. After hearing that story, Magnolia had invited Atlas for a ride on her back around the garden. But he wasn't interested.

Magnolia watched her father through the window, sipping a mug of hot tea. Mama Moon was stretched out beside him, reading a newspaper and eating a chocolate peppermint. And although they looked content, the rings around their eyes seemed even darker than before.

What Daddy needs for his birthday, thought Magnolia, *is an exotic holiday.* The baby would be here in a few months, and her parents had gone on holiday before she had arrived. She had seen the pictures. Mama Moon wearing her big floppy hat on the beach. Daddy Moon drinking from a coconut with a tiny umbrella inside. They looked so happy.

If Daddy Moon could go on an exotic holiday, he could take afternoon naps, eat different food, meet new people and try something he had never tried before. (Which was what Grandma Moon said exotic holidays were all about.) But holidays were expensive, and she knew what Mama Moon would say. There was a clatter and a crash as Atlas inched along the garden wall, knocking the lids off the bins.

Then Magnolia's toes tingled. Her eyes glowed. Maybe they didn't need to go anywhere to have a holiday. Maybe they could have one right here at number 84. The garden seemed suddenly alive, *listening*. The flowers nodded and bobbed. And the moon swayed gently in the autumn breeze, since it *was* a very good idea.

The next morning on her way to school, Magnolia went the long way down Applewhistle Lane. She stopped by the paddock to watch a bird sitting on the back of Tobias, the old one-eyed Clydesdale horse that belonged to Mr Washington. Magnolia watched as Tobias and the bird walked to the rusty claw-footed bath that he used as a water trough. She loved his long feathery fetlocks and pink whiskery nose.

The fence was rough and splintered. As she ran her fingers along the timber, Magnolia realized that she had been so busy planning her father's secret escape last night that she had forgotten all about Lost and Found. Today it was her turn to bring something to share with the class. Last week, Casper Sloan had brought custard apples that he had found on their tree, and Peggy Small had brought a tooth that she had lost.

She looked around, hoping to find a curious flower or seedpod. Then she noticed a crooked horseshoe hanging on the fence. Perfect. Magnolia put it in her bag. Then she hesitated. *Would Mr Washington mind? Mr Washington noticed everything.* Deciding it was better to ask, Magnolia walked up the creaky steps to his house. But as she knocked on the door,

Magnolia thought of a second question to ask Mr Washington.

When Magnolia got home from school that day, she looked for Mama Moon.

"Can I please invite Casper Sloan over on Saturday?"

"Of course," she said. "I always enjoy seeing Casper, and your father has never met him before."

Exactly, Magnolia thought, and she checked yet another thing off her list.

On Saturday, Casper Sloan arrived at eleven.

And just as Magnolia had planned, Casper had some custard apples like the ones he had brought for Lost and Found.

"Hello, Casper," said Daddy Moon, stretching out his hand. "It's nice to meet you."

"Gosh, what are those?" said Mama Moon, taking one of the fruits from Casper. "Are they pineapples?"

"Incorrect," said Casper. "They're custard apples. We have heaps on our tree."

"I've never tried a custard apple before," said Daddy Moon, touching the fruit's scaly skin. "They look like tiny dinosaurs."

"They're sort of slimy," said Casper. "But tasty."

Daddy Moon smiled and was about to sit down at his desk when Magnolia grabbed him by the arm and tugged him outside.

"Where are we going?" he said, looking hesitantly at the jungle of weeds and tangled branches they were heading for at the bottom of the garden.

"To an exotic place," said Magnolia. "And you can't walk to it, you have to ride."

"Ride?"

Before he could ask any more questions, two pointy ears poked over the fence.

Magnolia opened the gate. Mr Washington

was waiting with Tobias, right on time.

"Ever tried riding bareback on a one-eyed Clydesdale before?" grinned Mr Washington.

"Can't say that I have," said Daddy Moon, grinning back. Daddy Moon loved horses.

Magnolia found a milk crate for him to stand on. Atlas hissed. And Mama Moon laughed so much as she watched Daddy Moon trying to swing a leg over Tobias's back that you couldn't even see the rings around her eyes.

After Daddy Moon had managed to steer Tobias around the clothes line twice, he lay on the cushions that Magnolia had scattered in the jungle, rubbing his bruised bottom.

Magnolia took out a small parcel wrapped in newspaper.

"What's this for?" said Daddy Moon.

"No reason," said Magnolia.

Daddy Moon unwrapped the parcel and admired his new horseshoe.

"For good luck!" he said holding it up. "Although I feel pretty lucky already."

And then for no reason at all, Magnolia lit a candle on top of the custard apple and Mama Moon and Casper Sloan and Mr Washington sang *Happy Saturday* and *For He's a Jolly Great Clydesdale*.

Then Mama Moon put on her big floppy hat and was so relaxed that she didn't even seem to mind the bag of snowdrop bulbs that Mr Washington had brought as a present. And Daddy Moon spent the rest of the afternoon napping, eating different food, chatting to his new friend Casper, and trying not to fall off Tobias in the most exotic location in Thistledown.

It was their best holiday yet, and it hadn't cost a thing.

Mama Moon winked.

Magnolia winked back.

Chapter 5:

The Secret Something

The baby would be here any day. Magnolia Moon tiptoed down the hall. She could hear her parents talking downstairs. They were packing Mama's bag for hospital and whispering secret somethings. It was the third bag they had packed this week. It seemed the baby couldn't make up its mind, and they had already had two false starts.

Placing a toe on the top stair of the wooden spiral staircase, she slowly lowered her whole foot on the cold timber. It coughed loudly and gave her away.

"Magnolia?" called her mother.

"Back to bed, please," called her father.

"Tattle-tale," she hissed, taking her foot off the stair.

"Sneak!" it hissed back.

Magnolia wondered what she had done to the staircase, what it had seen or heard that had made it plot against her. At most times of the day, Magnolia could pass up and down the stairs without it making a peep. Not a crack or a quiver. But whenever she was trying to sneak past to overhear a conversation, it always knew what she was up to and it would creak and groan and spoil everything. It wasn't easy being nine and a half.

In the morning, Magnolia went to get into her parents' bed. Except the indigo sheets were empty; the stars in a tangle. She wanted to scooch between them and listen to Mama singing.

Everything would be different now. A sad

little tune strummed the strings of her heart.

"Mama?" she called out.

No answer.

"Daddy?"

Silence.

Then there was a rustle from the kitchen.

"Atlas?"

"Yodel-Ay-Hee-Hoo!"

Magnolia grinned. Grandma Moon was here.

"Aha!" said Grandma Moon, squatting down on the side of the road. "Blue-banded bee, and fast asleep, too."

Magnolia leaned in. It was the most beautiful bee she had ever seen. With a fluffy golden mane, green eyes and crinkly cellophane wings the colour of coffee. And all along its glossy black abdomen were bright turquoise stripes making it look just like one of Grandma Moon's liquorice allsorts.

"It's a solitary bee that makes a nest instead of living in a hive."

Grandma Moon sank onto the dirt, plucked a pencil from her straw hat and started sketching wildly in her notebook. Grandma Moon was an amateur entomologist, which Magnolia had learned was a fancy way of saying that Grandma Moon liked learning about insects and the environment.

Walking to school with Grandma Moon was one of Magnolia's favourite things to do. It always took three times as long, and they were always late. But the best thing of all was going to stay with Grandma Moon and her noisy family. There was her blackbird called Figaro, her cats, Tristan and Isolde ... and her pig, Madame Butterfly.

Grandma Moon adored Madame Butterfly. Once Magnolia had even found the pig asleep in Grandma Moon's bed while Grandma Moon slept on a cushion on the hard wooden floor.

"Poor thing was out of spirits," she had said. "Fancied a bit of pampering."

"Couldn't you have shared?" Magnolia had asked.

"We tried," she said. "But she kept stealing the blankets. Don't call 'em hogs for nothing!"

And she had snorted and slapped her knees and laughed so hard that a button popped off and rolled across the floor.

"Will the baby come home today?" Magnolia asked now as they reached the iron gates of Thistledown Preparatory.

"Perhaps," said Grandma. "Or tomorrow. Babies have a way of making their own plans."

Magnolia was getting a little tired of hearing this.

Then Grandma Moon froze, her nose in the air. Magnolia knew this was just Grandma Moon "sharpening her senses".

"Shh," said Grandma Moon. "Listen."

"What is it?" said Magnolia, wrapping her rainbow scarf tighter around her neck.

"The wind," said Grandma Moon. "It's telling you a secret."

Magnolia looked to the winter sky. Something about it had changed. It drummed and fizzed with life. She listened closely, separating each buzz, click and chirrup. All around, things were travelling home, searching for a place to land.

Magnolia's toes tingled. Her eyes glowed.

The baby will come home today, thought Magnolia. *The baby's here.*

Magnolia Moon stared at her watch. Ten o'clock. *Still.* She blew on the watch hands – trying to coax them forwards. They didn't budge.

"What's the time?" Magnolia whispered to Casper Sloan. Mr Hawkins had paused his lesson to help Adrian March, who had stapled his shoelaces together by accident.

"Ten o'clock," said Casper. "Is your watch broken?"

"No," said Magnolia. "I was just hoping that yours said something different."

Magnolia sighed, her knees jiggling impatiently under the desk. There were five more hours until the end of school, which was a lifetime if you were a sandcastle.

She stared out the window at the empty playground. The Year Six students would be coming out for morning tea soon. They always got to go out first. Then something caught her eye.

The playground wasn't empty. There was a statue on the edge of the oval. A long shadow stretched upon the grass. Then the statue moved. Magnolia stood up, her heart bouncing in her chest as she recognized the tall, willowy figure; the graceful arch of his neck, the spidery sweep of his hair.

"All right, you lot," said Mr Hawkins, jolting Magnolia from her reverie. "You're welcome to go. Just pick up one piece of rubbish from the classroom on your way out."

There was a laugh behind her as Peggy Small

and Wren Snow dived for the same cardboard box on the floor.

"Excuse me," said Magnolia to Mr Hawkins, who was coming past with the broom. "Do you know who that boy is?"

Mr Hawkins squinted at the window.

"That's Reuben," he said. "He's just joined Year Six."

"Reuben," repeated Magnolia softly. The name felt smooth and stretchy like a noodle.

She picked up a strip of paper and some pencil shavings from the floor then returned to the window to watch.

"Ready," whispered Magnolia, seeing Reuben raise his arms and tilt his chin to the sky.

"Steady ..." she said as he crouched, drawing himself back like an arrow in a bow.

"Magnolia?" said Casper, standing at the door.

"Coming," she said, waving to her friend.

But when she turned back, Reuben was gone.

Then she saw him. A white smudge on the horizon.

Running. Flying.

Like an angel.

When the school bell rang at the end of the day, Magnolia *ran*. Zooming through the waist-high grass behind the school, Magnolia didn't notice the burn in her shins, the dampness in her shoes or the thorns snagging her knuckles. On she went, skidding over moss-covered rocks and stumps, tussling with fallen branches. She imagined that she was racing Reuben, mounted high on the back of Pegasus, the giant winged stallion on the cover of her book of Greek myths. Magnolia gripped her legs around the horse-god's broad back as he reared and pawed the sky.

As they soared along Chimneypot Parade towards 84 Crocus Cottage, Magnolia saw Grandma Moon's cowboy boots sticking out of the vegetable patch. She was putting a caterpillar *into* the broccoli instead of taking it out. Grandma

Moon didn't believe in the food chain and thought that caterpillars deserved a good meal as much as anybody else. Which was why there were never any vegetables to eat at Grandma Moon's; the insects got them all, which was just fine with Magnolia.

"Are they here?" Magnolia yelled from the front gate.

"See for yourself," said Grandma Moon, grinning and waving her hat.

Magnolia hurled her bag onto the floor and flew up the staircase.

"Stop!" it croaked.

"I can't!" she yelled, leaning against Pegasus's neck, his white mane whipping her face.

Then she heard a song. Magnolia stopped. She knew it well. It was the secret song that had been playing in her heart since the day she found out she was going to be a big sister. Except it wasn't in her heart any more. It was coming from Mama and Daddy Moon.

She followed the tune down the hall to her parents' bedroom. She peered in. They were singing it to a small yellow bundle cradled between them. They were singing *her* song. Her special song! The one about the little moon. And Magnolia didn't feel like flying any more.

"Come and say hello," said Mama, patting the indigo sheets dotted with stars. Magnolia couldn't. Besides, there was no room on the bed for her to sit. No room in the sky for another Moon.

"Meet Finnegan."

Magnolia took a step closer. From the bookcase she could see that the bundle had a tiny nose, soft plump cheeks and a spray of fine eyelashes like the fronds of a fern.

"Would you like to hold him?"

Magnolia wasn't sure.

So Mama shuffled to the left. Daddy shuffled to the right. And Magnolia swam across the stars to find her spot. The bed fit all four of them perfectly. Each with their own place in the universe. Mama Moon on the left. Daddy Moon on the right. And Magnolia in the middle with Finnegan on her lap: a bright-yellow bundle lighting up the sky. He smelled of moss and summer rain. She took his tiny hand in hers, his fingers curling around her thumb, then she joined in singing the song. She could teach him the words. And how to climb trees. And how to write his name backwards. And where to find blue-banded bees. And how to dance the Heel and Toe Polka up the hill and through the streets of Thistledown. Everything would be different now. But maybe some things would never change.

Then Magnolia leaned down and whispered a secret something in his ear.

And although it flashed across his dark shining eyes like a rippling wave, he didn't make a sound.

Since Finnegan Moon was very good at keeping secrets.

Chapter 6:

The Secret Spook

Magnolia Moon has yellow daisies on her new curtains. It was the moon that saw them first. Along with the gap in her teeth when she poked her head through the top window of 84 Crocus Cottage. But that is a secret. Imogen May is sure she saw them first.

The moon and the girl are often whispering. On the tops of hills. On the ends of beds, where they try not to giggle and wake her dribbly brother Finnegan, asleep down the hall. They like all the same things, such as peeking through windows and sneaking through shadows to overhear important conversations; neither one being afraid of the dark. And much like the moon, Magnolia has many faces. Both are good at impressions. You never know what they might be. Just this week they have been a rabbit, a beetle, a fox, a bear, a lion and a toad, depending on whom you ask. But if you ask Magnolia, she will not tell you, or even Imogen May.

"There is a ghost in my house," said Imogen May.

"A real one?" said Magnolia.

"I think so," said Imogen May, wrapping herself in one of Magnolia's new bedroom curtains.

"How do you know?"

"I can hear it. Every night there is a shuffle in the hallway and a white flash past my door."

"Have you tried to catch it?"

"Not yet," sighed Imogen May. "Too spooky. I wish I had yellow daisies on my curtains.

Our curtains are old and brown and horrible. No wonder there are ghosts hiding behind them."

Magnolia nodded. She didn't believe in ghosts. Although if she did, an old, brown curtain would be the first place she would go looking. In the morning she would ask her parents if she and Imogen May could have a second sleepover next Friday night. That way, she could see for herself. Right now, though, there were more important matters to discuss.

"I would be a dragon fruit," said Magnolia, dangling upside-down from her bed.

"Do they breathe fire?" said Imogen May, swinging beside her.

"Yes."

"I would be an apple," said Imogen May.

"Why?" said Magnolia, tickling Atlas under his chin.

"Because you are constantly reinventing yourself. You are always doing something new. Apple jam, apple pie, apple sauce, apple cake. Apples can be anything."

"Or you could be left in the bottom of a smelly schoolbag and forgotten about because everyone is sick of you."

"Actually, can I change my answer?"

"No, you can't."

When Magnolia woke up, Mama Moon was pacing up and down the hallway patting Finnegan on the bottom and doing funny bouncy squats. He was doing the woolly-bleaty-lamb-cry that he did when he was just about to go to sleep. Magnolia preferred this to the angry-screechy-cockatoo-cry he did when he had sore teeth, which was most days.

Magnolia got the breakfast things out and put an extra piece of toast in for Imogen May. Then she decided to give it to Mama Moon, as rhubarb jam might put her in the mood for agreeing to a second sleepover.

Magnolia left the buttery triangles at the bottom of the wooden spiral staircase.

"Watch it!" the staircase barked.

"Oh, shush!" Magnolia hissed back.

The staircase had been in a foul mood ever since Finnegan had been born, due to all the bouncy squats occurring in the middle of the night. It croaked and grumbled even more than usual during Magnolia's late-night sneaks, determined to give her away and stop her from overhearing important conversations.

"The answer is yes," said Mama Moon, spying Magnolia loitering at the foot of the staircase.

"Pardon?"

"Imogen May has already asked me."

"Thank you, Mama!" Magnolia squealed, sliding the plate off the bottom stair and running into the kitchen.

"But leave the toast!"

On Friday, there was fish curry for dinner at the Bells' house. Magnolia loved the way their kitchen smelled, so full of herbs and spices. Magnolia watched as Mr Bell dropped golden threads of saffron into the steaming pot bubbling with cinnamon, cumin and cardamom pods. Magnolia ate every bit of her curry and had a second scoop of coconut rice to soak up the sauce. And then she ate the rest of Ernest's, Imogen May's four-year-old brother, who didn't want his.

When it was time for bed, Magnolia listened to the sound of the wind chimes hanging from a pipe on their garden shed.

"The best way to get rid of a ghost is to give it a fright. Then it won't come back," said Imogen May.

"How do you do that?"

"Everyone is afraid of something. It's just a matter of finding out what."

"What are you afraid of?" asked Magnolia.

Imogen May thought for a moment. "Smoked oysters, cherry-flavoured cough medicine and trigonometry."

"Me too," Magnolia grimaced. "And Mrs Eggers."

Imogen May winced at the memory of her old neighbour from Chimneypot Parade.

They shivered together for a while until the room grew still and a light snore came from Imogen May's direction.

But Magnolia couldn't sleep. The moon was at the window. She waved hello and was about to poke her head out and tell it all her news, when there was a shuffle in the hallway. A white flash past the door.

"Imogen May," squeaked Magnolia. "Imogen May, wake up! It's the ghost!"

But Imogen May only mumbled something about apples and rolled over.

Magnolia was alone. She would have to catch the secret spook by herself.

She tiptoed out of the bedroom and through the living room. She inched through the inky black; the room a dark, swirling sea, each couch a towering rock. Feeling her way, she imagined she was in a boat sailing through a narrow channel.

Magnolia wondered what lurked beneath those rocks. Was that where Charybdis lived? The sea monster with the gaping mouth and uncontrollable thirst for the sea that she had found in her book of Greek myths. Charybdis lived beneath a small rock only an arrowshot away from Scylla, another sea monster living inside a bigger rock.

In the dark, Magnolia could hear them taunting and teasing, forcing her to find a safe passage

between them. But as she steered away from one of them, she was steering right into the grip of the other.

When she reached the kitchen, she heard a whimper and a rustle. It was coming from behind one of the curtains. Magnolia followed it. Then there was a howling whistle from the midnight train outside, and she swung the curtain open. Magnolia yelped with surprise as the ghost flew past her. Then it stopped and turned around. She stared into its haunted eyes. They were wide and frightened. It was breathing hard. It was wearing white robot pyjamas.

"Ernest?"

When Ernest had finally caught his breath, he huddled beside Magnolia in the shadowy hall.

"Is there something you want to tell me?" said Magnolia.

Ernest nodded.

"Is it a secret?"

Ernest nodded again, glancing nervously at the bathroom.

Magnolia leaned in.

"I don't like the flushing sound the toilet makes. It's ... scary."

"It is," agreed Magnolia. "But it doesn't *mean* to be. It can't help it, just like Mrs Eggers."

"Does she make horrible gurgly sounds too?"

"Sometimes. When you step on her garden. You simply need to be brave and take charge. I tell her: *Mrs Eggers, I am going to walk past your house now and I promise to stay off your petunias, if you promise to stay where you are.*"

Ernest chewed his thumbnail.

"Besides," said Magnolia. "You're a robot. I bet you can make some funny sounds right back if you have to."

Magnolia took Ernest by the hand and led him back into the bathroom. She switched on the light.

"Good evening," said Magnolia, "my name is Magnolia Moon. I have a brother called Finnegan, a cat called Atlas and a new tooth coming through. I live at 84 Crocus Cottage, where we have a toilet a lot like you. I am going to flush you now, and you are going to get on with it and not make a fuss."

Magnolia looked to Ernest. "Anything you would like to add?"

"Maybe something like you said before ... about staying where it is."

Magnolia nodded pertly.

"And you are to stay there, and you are not, I repeat *not*, to follow us down the hall."

Ernest giggled. "It can't *really* hear you, can it?"

"Of course not." Magnolia giggled too. "Like Mrs Eggers." Because in truth Magnolia was far too afraid of her and only whispered it as she tiptoed past her house on Chimneypot Parade.

Magnolia pressed the button. There was a whoosh and a gurgle.

"The toilet's not real. It's just a bunch of smelly pipes with a job to do."

Then she gave Ernest a gentle nudge. "You try."

So Ernest introduced himself then set down the rules. He was firm but fair. And this time when he flushed the toilet, instead of running into the living room and hiding behind a curtain, Ernest whispered robot sounds all the way back to his bed.

As Magnolia waited for him to fall asleep, she wondered if she might one day tuck her own brother Finnegan into bed and kiss him goodnight. She hoped she would.

"I scared away the ghost!" announced Imogen May at breakfast.

Felix blew a raspberry. Ernest nibbled on his toast.

"When?" said Magnolia.

"Last night, when you were asleep," said Imogen May. "I put a tin of smoked oysters behind the curtain in the living room."

"Did you see it?"

"Yup. It was hairy and enormous, a lot like a spotted crocapus, and I told it to buzz off."

"Well done!" said Magnolia, although she knew that spotted crocapuses were actually quite small and happened to love smoked oysters.

"It was pretty scary."

"Everybody gets scared sometimes," said Magnolia.

"By the way, did you know you snore?" said Imogen May.

"I was having a dream about a robot."

"What sort of robot?"

"A cool one," said Magnolia. "Brave, too."

"I like robots," said Imogen May.

"So do I," said Magnolia.

Ernest's toes tingled. His eyes glowed.

He grinned at Magnolia.

Magnolia grinned back.

Chapter 7:

The Secret Identity

Snip, snip, snip, went the scissors. *Slurp, slurp, slurp,* went Mama Moon on her straw as she *swish, swish, swish*ed through the pages of her glossy magazine.

Magnolia Moon loved coming along to see her mother getting a haircut. She wondered what it would be like to sit on the tall puffy seat and have somebody ask her important questions. Grandma Moon always cut her hair. She would sit on a kitchen stool with a tea towel around her shoulders while Grandma Moon told her about Goliath stick insects and Hercules moths. And when she reached the exciting parts, her glasses would fog up and she would forget which direction she was snipping.

Today, it was Magnolia's job to distract Finnegan when he went red in the face, fed up from waiting. She had already tried jiggling his buggy, wiggling his elephant and waggling her tongue. But it wasn't working.

"You can take him outside for a walk if you like?" suggested Mama Moon. "Just to the clock tower and back."

Magnolia and Finnegan scooted out of the

salon and down the street. Magnolia loved the busy hum of the town square in the morning, like an orchestra getting ready to perform. Everybody was tuning up, looking for the right note to play. When they reached the town hall, Magnolia parked Finnegan beneath the old astral clock. The ancient dials lurched to show the position of the sun and the moon in the sky. They stared in awe at the golden figures decorating the clock: the roaring lion, the strutting peacock and the bellowing cow. But it was starting to rain, so Magnolia took Finnegan back to the salon. Mama Moon was paying at the counter.

When she had finished, she dropped a silver coin into the tip jar. A woman with sparkly earrings waved to Magnolia. Magnolia waved back.

"When will I be big enough to get my hair cut on my own?" said Magnolia as they ran through the rain to the car.

"Grandma Moon does an excellent job," said Mama Moon. "Except for that one time ..." Mama Moon trailed off.

"And that *other* time..." said Magnolia.

"Oh, yes."

When they had returned to 84 Crocus Cottage and unpacked their groceries, Magnolia sat at the kitchen table and got out her pencils. She was going to write a letter to Imogen May. But she felt somebody watching her. Mama Moon was standing behind her, inspecting her hair as though Magnolia was a chimp being groomed.

"You know..." said her mother, plucking a

feather and a string of ivy from her hair. "You really are such a responsible girl. And you could do with a bit of a trim. It's a wonder you can see anything."

Magnolia sensed where this was going and began to make small cheeping noises and little mews.

"So perhaps you could go along on your own and have a proper haircut."

Her small cheeps and mews turned to loud hooting sounds as Magnolia pushed her chair back and hugged her mother.

"All right, all right," said Mama Moon. "I'll make an appointment."

"Ooh, ooh, ooh," hooted Magnolia, beating her chest.

Magnolia swung her legs under the tall puffy seat.

"Can I get you anything while you wait?" said the woman with sparkly earrings.

Magnolia was sure she would like something,

but didn't know what to ask for. The woman smiled kindly.

"A glass of water, perhaps? A magazine?"

"Yes please," said Magnolia.

There was something about being alone on a Wednesday afternoon in a hairdressing salon that made Magnolia feel taller and wiser and not a bit like Magnolia Moon. As she looked at her reflection in the mirror, she saw somebody else entirely staring back.

Then a man appeared beside her. He had a curly moustache that turned up at the corners and a trolley full of bottles and combs.

"Good afternoon, Madame," said the man. "My name is Frank, and I will be cutting your hair today."

"Hello, Frank," said Magnolia, extending a hand. "My name is Violet Winter."

Snip, snip, snip, went the scissors. *Slurp, slurp, slurp,* went Violet Winter on her straw as she

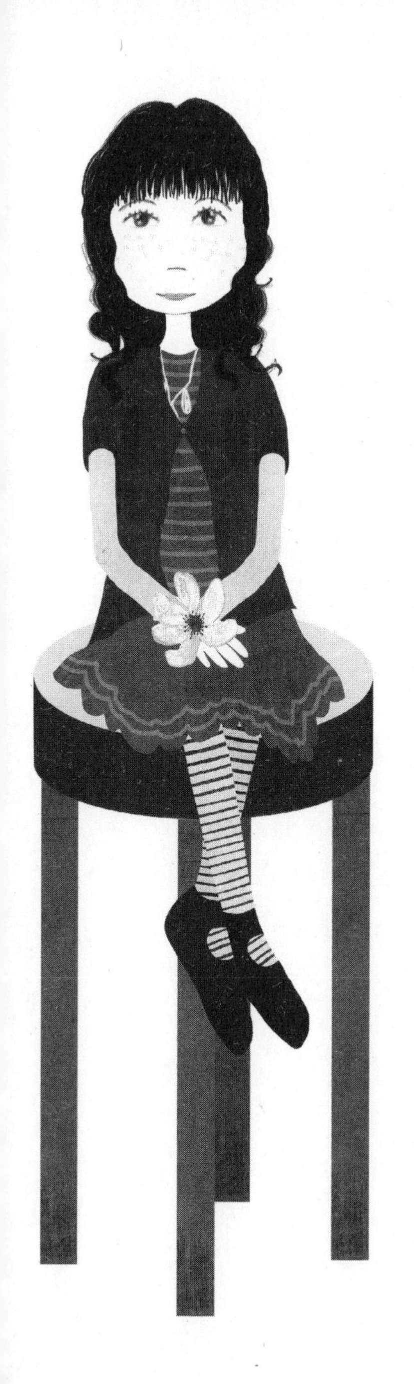

*swish, swish, swish*ed through the pages of her glossy magazine.

"Have you had a nice day?" said Frank. "The weather has been unseasonably warm."

"Unseasonably," agreed Violet. "I took off my scarf as soon as I got to school."

Although, in truth, it had really been a jumper – but a scarf sounded much more important.

"Yes, you need to wear layers, don't you? Are you enjoying school?"

Violet nodded.

"How are you liking ... let's see, Year Five, Year Six?"

Violet's tummy tumbled; nobody had ever mistaken her for an eleven-year-old before.

"Year Six," she said before she could catch the words jumping out of her mouth.

"How wonderful," said Frank. "At Thistledown Preparatory?"

Violet nodded.

"I walk there on my own from 84 Crocus Cottage," she said, which also wasn't true, although she *would* be walking on her own once she was eleven so it was *almost* true.

"You'd know my son Reuben, then? He's new to the school. He's in Year Six too. Just turned eleven, yet he's already taller than I am. I will ask him to keep an eye out for you."

Magnolia glanced at the mirror. She did not feel like Violet Winter any more. She felt small and foolish and she wanted to go home.

Magnolia Moon saw Reuben three times that week. The flying boy. The angel boy. When he ran across the playground each day, he looked so grand and graceful that Magnolia thought he really would take off and fly away. Now, more than ever, Magnolia wanted to fly with him through that secret sky. She almost had a few times, had got all the way to the edge of the oval when something inside stopped her. She could never fly with him now. Not now he would find out that she was just a silly, fibbing nine-year-old that couldn't be trusted even if she *did* have a very nice haircut.

As she lay in bed, Magnolia imagined Frank coming home and asking Reuben if there was a girl called Violet Winter in his class.

"Violet Winter?" he would say. "There's no such person."

Frank would scratch his head and pinch the corners of his moustache.

"But I met her today. She lives at 84 Crocus Cottage."

"Oh," the angel boy would sigh. "*That* girl... I've seen her before. But she is just a baby in Year Four."

And they would laugh and laugh and laugh. And then Frank would tell the woman with the sparkly earrings. And the woman would laugh too and tell Mama Moon next time she got her hair cut. And Mama Moon would tell Daddy Moon and her mouth would go all thin and his eyebrows would go all crooked because she was in fact *not* a responsible girl and they were disappointed that they had raised a daughter who told lies. And she would pack her bag and kiss Finnegan goodbye and leave home since she would not be welcome at 84 Crocus Cottage any more. And she would have to live on an island and eat wild currants and catch her own sardines for dinner. And she didn't like sardines.

When Magnolia came home from school on Friday, everything felt heavy. Her shoulders, her bag, her feet. It had been raining all day and the garden seemed thicker and wilder than it had been this morning. She plopped down on the front step and squeezed water out of her socks. Mama Moon was doing bouncy squats up and down the stairs with Finnegan.

"Umph," wheezed the staircase.

"I'm going to the hairdresser's this afternoon," said Mama Moon. "Do you want to come?"

Magnolia's stomach dropped.

"Again?" said Magnolia. "You only went last week."

"Yes, I'm not sure I like this colour. It's a bit ... loud."

"No, thank you," said Magnolia.

Mama Moon stopped squatting and poked her head around the door. Then she walked over and put the back of her palm against Magnolia's forehead.

"That's not like you," said Mama Moon. "Are you feeling all right? You don't feel hot."

"I'm fine," said Magnolia. "I just don't feel like it."

"Well, I'm sorry, but it wasn't so much of an invitation as a warning. You are going to have to come with me as I need you to look after Finnegan. Take him out for a walk when he starts to cry. He won't sit still for that long."

Magnolia stayed close to her mother's side as she walked through the salon door. She scanned the shop. No sign of Frank. Magnolia let her insides go soft again. The woman with the sparkly earrings greeted them at the desk.

"Come this way," she said, leading them to the sinks with funny little hoses.

Magnolia relaxed and pushed Finnegan's buggy to a row of empty seats.

Then Frank walked past with a trolley.

"Hello, Violet," he called.

Magnolia winced and waved hello. Her mother didn't seem to have noticed.

"I might take Finnegan for a walk," said Magnolia.

"It's raining."

"It's only light," said Magnolia.

Mama Moon raised her eyebrows as the rain clattered on the roof.

Magnolia sighed and took Finnegan across to a large pot plant, as far away from Frank as she could get, where she pretended to read a brochure about shampoo.

Then she heard the *squeak, squeak, squeak*

of footsteps. And the *sweep, sweep, sweep* of a broom. *Frank's* broom.

Magnolia pushed her chin deeper into her chest and stared at the pictures of shiny ponytails.

Thud, thud, thud, went her heart.

"Listen to that rain!" said Frank, making a neat pile of hair clippings. "My quince tree will be happy."

Frank nodded at Finnegan.

"Happy little chap, isn't he?"

Magnolia smiled shyly. He went on sweeping, doing a lap of the whole salon.

"By the way, I asked my boy to look out for you," said Frank. "But he didn't know of anyone with your name."

Outside, the astral clock chimed. She imagined the skeletons shaking their heads in disappointment.

Magnolia's cheeks burned. A red blotchy patch began to darken on her chest.

"Still that's not surprising," continued Frank. "Reuben's a shy boy and doesn't talk to many people. Do say hello if you see him. It is hard making new friends."

Magnolia couldn't bear it any more.

"Can I tell you a secret?" said Magnolia.

"If you like," said Frank.

Squeak. Squeak. Squeak.

"I'm not really eleven ... I'm nine and three quarters. Your son is two years above me."

Sweep. Sweep. Sweep.

"And my name is not really Violet."

Frank stopped sweeping.

Magnolia stared at her toes. She wondered whether it was too late to climb inside the pot or whether the pot would fit on her head?

Frank was still for a moment then he began sweeping again.

"Can I tell *you* a secret?" he said.

Magnolia nodded, still staring at her shoes.

Frank leaned in.

"I have a mouse in my pocket."

Magnolia's mouth fell open. She glanced at his coat pocket. There was a small lump in the corner.

"My wife put mouse traps down last night. Horrible things. There are mice all over our house and something needs to be done. But I found this one this morning as I was going to work and I just couldn't ... well, *look* at her."

Frank reached into his coat pocket and held up a mouse. She had sooty-brown fur and her ears and paws were the colour of musk sticks.

Snuffle, snuffle, snuffle, went her nose.

"I call her Charlotte."

Magnolia gazed at the mouse. She felt a weight fall away. She thought about the angel boy. She felt so light that she thought she might lift off the ground and grow wings, too. Tomorrow she would fly with Reuben: cross her final goal off her list in her secret envelope. They would fly across the playground, over the iron gates and Mr Hawkins's green bicycle. Climbing up and up on ladders of sky. She would glide above chimneys and rooftops, across fields and copses all the way to Imogen May's. Then back home across the ocean, where she would race with the moon, over silver cliffs and craggy waves, dirt lanes and stone walls. Waving to her grandma and Madame Butterfly, Mr Washington and old Tobias. Past Casper and Bonnie, and the Wishing Tree. She would land in Chimneypot Parade, careful not to squash Mrs Eggers's petunias, and run around the corner to 84 Crocus Cottage where she would tell Finnegan and Atlas all about it.

"Hello, Charlotte," she said, running a finger across the mouse's silky cheek. "My name is Magnolia Moon."

Chapter 8:

The Secret Sky

It was lunchtime.

"What have you got?" said Magnolia Moon, peering hungrily into Casper Sloan's brown paper bag. It was only Tuesday, but Magnolia felt hungry enough for Wednesday's and Thursday's lunch too. Plus a hot chocolate.

"Try and guess," said Casper.

Casper Sloan always brought interesting lunches to school. He packed them himself, making sure that each item of food matched a different letter of the alphabet every day.

Yesterday had been the letter "M". He'd brought mushroom soup, macadamia nuts, muesli bars and malted milk biscuits.

Magnolia poked at the bag. It was lumpy.

"Give me a clue."

"Today's letter is the letter 'W'."

"W" was a good letter. A lot of Magnolia's favourite things started with "W".

A poem began to take shape:

Whales. Waves. Winter seas.

Water lilies. Willow trees.

Wrapping paper. Witches' spells.

Windy days. Wishing wells.

"Windmills. Wind chimes. Wheelbarrows..." chanted Magnolia. Then she stopped, since her throat felt scratchy and she couldn't find a word to rhyme with wheelbarrows. Except for perhaps "old marrows", which she didn't like at all, and they didn't start with "W".

Casper was waiting, so Magnolia scrunched up her eyes and tried to think of food that began with the letter "W". It was making her mouth water.

"Wontons with wasabi, then waffles with white chocolate and watermelon?"

"Incorrect," said Casper and he took out each item and set it out on the grass. "Watercress on white bread, walnut cake and wheatgrass juice."

Magnolia was impressed. Then he pulled out a pear.

"That's cheating," said Magnolia. "Pear starts with 'P'!"

Casper gazed calmly at Magnolia.

"It's a *Williams* pear," he said, "so it counts. What about you?"

Magnolia peered in her lunchbox. She didn't have any of those things. Only an egg and pickle sandwich. Again. Because the hen next door kept laying and Daddy Moon kept pickling: cucumbers, cauliflowers, radishes, aubergines – anything he could find.

"Can I tell you a secret?" said Magnolia, her eyes fixed firmly on the oval.

Casper nodded.

"I am going to fly today!"

Casper looked sceptical.

"I tried that once," said Casper. "I jumped out of the big tree in my front garden. It hurt."

Magnolia laughed and licked the icing off the walnut cake, wondering whether it was also cheating to have caramel icing, since caramel started with the letter "C".

She kept watching the oval, waiting for the tall shadow of Reuben to fall across the grass. Today she would run with him. She would fly through his secret sky. She wondered what she would say. What he would say. What did you say to an angel? Magnolia sat and thought about this, never once taking her eyes off the oval, in case Reuben should appear.

But then the bell rang. Casper sneezed. And Reuben never came.

"Are you coming to science?" said Casper, blowing his nose on a stripey handkerchief.

Magnolia stood reluctantly and followed Casper back to class, scanning the lines outside the Year Six classrooms for any sign of Reuben. He wasn't there.

He must be sick, thought Magnolia. *I will have to fly tomorrow.*

But that was a lifetime if you were a mayfly or one of Mama Moon's newspapers.

When Magnolia Moon woke up the next day, a thought hatched from her head like a spring chicken. *It's today!* The day she was going to fly with Reuben. Then the fuzzy yellow chick staggered to the right and sneezed. Magnolia swung her legs out of bed, and her head hurt, her throat hurt and her belly gurgled. Magnolia Moon was sick.

Atlas padded across the end of her quilt and stared out the window. The yellow daisies on her curtains seemed to droop. Outside, the world buzzed with possibility: gate latches snapped, doors thudded, hedgers snipped, leads jangled, claws clicked, heels clacked and strands of laughter floated by. The Minks, the Snows, the Lawsons, Polly Eggers and everybody from Chimneypot Parade was going somewhere. Even the moon was out and it was half past eight in the morning. Magnolia grabbed a handful of tissues and shivered sadly to herself as she climbed back under the covers.

Then there was a knock on the door and Daddy Moon crept in with a mug of hot chocolate and a fresh pair of pyjamas.

"Ah," he whispered. "You're awake."

"I'm late for school," said Magnolia, fumbling with the covers. Her father gently patted them down and took her temperature.

"You had a fever all night, so you're staying home today."

"But I will miss ... science."

"Science?" said Daddy Moon.

Magnolia nodded. She had wanted to say "flying with an angel", but she said "science" instead. Although it *was* true, she would miss science.

Daddy Moon cleared a space among the scrunched-up tissues on the end of her bed and sat down. Magnolia took the mug in her hands. It was warm. *Too* warm. A marshmallow bobbed on the top. She poked at it, pushed it under the chocolate foam. It bounced back up again. Her belly gurgled, and she pushed it away. Magnolia always liked hot chocolate. This was *serious.*

"What are you studying in science?"

"The water cycle," croaked Magnolia.

"Ah," said Daddy Moon. His hands felt cool and soothing against her forehead. She lifted her arms helpfully as he peeled off her damp pyjamas and put on a new pair.

"It's like this," said Daddy Moon, rolling up his sleeves. "The sun heats up the water from rivers, lakes and oceans and turns it into steam like a great big kettle!"

Magnolia looked outside at the sun. It didn't seem like a kettle.

"And when the steam travels up and up into the sky, it turns into clouds."

His cheeks were flushed pink with excitement. Daddy Moon was heating up too.

"If enough steam goes up, the clouds get so heavy that they turn grey and fall apart! And what do you think they turn into?"

"Rain?" croaked Magnolia, remembering the curly picture Mr Hawkins had drawn on the board. "And hail and snow."

"See?" said Daddy Moon. "Nothing to it. Now try to get some rest."

Magnolia listened to her father's footsteps going down the stairs and out into the garden. It was his one day off all month, and she was stuck in bed. He would probably spend the whole morning out there on his hands and knees with Mama Moon and Finnegan. Out there planting seeds and digging up weeds. There would be worms and ladybirds, finches and mossy stones. And Mama Moon would be laughing so much beneath her big, floppy hat that she would forget to be cross about the patch of snowdrops that had cropped up beneath the orange tree.

As Magnolia stared at the blue sky, dotted with tiny white puffs of clouds, she imagined Reuben flying through it without her, arms spread, chin high. She pictured Casper sitting alone at school taking out his lunch with nobody to guess the letter of the day. Magnolia rolled over. Her pyjamas felt stiff and scratchy. They were fresh off the line and smelled like sunshine. Magnolia scowled at her pyjamas – even they had been having fun outside without her. It just wasn't fair. She kicked at her sheets, her thoughts growing stormier still, since maybe she would never get better. Maybe she would never fly. Magnolia glared at those white puffs and tried to turn them grey. She wished that it *would* rain. At least if it was raining, then *everybody* would be inside and nobody would be able to fly without her – not even the birds.

"Imagine if you could make a cloud," she said to Atlas softly in the dim half-light. "If you could make your own secret sky."

Atlas turned away; he didn't like getting wet. Then her belly gurgled.

"Shush!" she said to it. "I'm trying to think."

But her belly took no notice of her.

Then Magnolia sat up. Her toes tingled. Her eyes glowed. Perhaps she *could* make a cloud. Could make it rain – make it *pour*. Daddy Moon had said there was nothing to it. Magnolia closed her eyes and pictured herself striding down

Chimneypot Parade holding a thunderbolt above her head just like Zeus, the "cloud gatherer" in her book of Greek myths. But the vision didn't last long, since she was quite sure that the king of the gods and ruler of the heavens had never once put down his thunderbolt to blow his nose.

Magnolia Moon woke.

"Rats!" she hissed, having wasted the whole morning in bed. She looked at the clock. It was eleven: there was still time. The lunch bell at school wouldn't ring for another hour, which was a lifetime if you were a storm cloud. She swung her legs out of bed and tried to stand up. Her knees wobbled. Everything hurt – even her pinky toes. She put on her dressing gown and slippers and hobbled into the empty kitchen. To make a cloud, Daddy Moon had said you needed something hot like the sun and something wet like the ocean. Magnolia opened the cupboard and took out the hottest things she could find: some dried red chillies, an onion, a red pepper, some curry powder, smoked paprika, peppercorns, a tin of red beans and the spicy sausage that Daddy Moon liked. She put them on the counter and chopped them up into tiny pieces. Then she grabbed her umbrella from the laundry, went back upstairs and ran a hot bath; the wettest thing she could think of.

While Magnolia waited for the bath to fill, she did a little rain dance and practised what she was going to say to Reuben. She had got as far as, "Hello," when she turned off the tap. Then she tossed in the hot things and stirred them together with a wooden spoon. Steam began to rise in a plume around her and the mirror in the bathroom fogged up. It was working! The spicy, steamy cloud rose up from the bath, making the coils in her hair curl up tighter. Magnolia opened the window and tried to tempt it out, pushing it up and up into the sky.

Outside in the garden below, Mama Moon raised her head and sniffed the air. Then Daddy

Moon and Finnegan did the same.

"What's that lovely smell?" said Daddy Moon, taking off his gardening gloves.

"I don't know," said Mama Moon, taking off her floppy hat. "It smells delicious."

So Mama Moon, Daddy Moon and Finnegan

followed the scent through the front door and up the wooden staircase. And when they found Magnolia perched on the edge of the bath beneath her umbrella, they didn't have time to ask her questions. Because the Minks, the Snows, the Lawsons, Polly Eggers and everybody from Chimneypot Parade was coming up the garden path, hoping to be invited in.

And for the first time all day, everyone was inside. Because Magnolia Moon had not made a cloud – however she *had* made some delicious hot soup. And once Magnolia had finished her bowl, she felt just well enough for a mug of hot chocolate.

As Magnolia walked to school on Friday, she practised what she was going to say to Reuben again. She had got as far as, "Hello, my name is Magnolia Moon," which wasn't very far at all. And by lunchtime, she hadn't got much further.

Magnolia peered into Casper Sloan's brown paper bag.

"What have you got?"

"Try to guess," said Casper.

Magnolia didn't have time to guess. A tall shadow had just fallen across the playground.

It was Reuben.

"Quick!" said Magnolia, jumping up and dragging Casper Sloan by the arm.

"Where are we going?" said Casper, stumbling on his shoelaces.

"You'll see!" said Magnolia, trying to remember her opening line.

But when Magnolia reached Reuben, she didn't have time to wonder what to say, as his arms were wide, his chin was high. She gazed up at him in awe. His eyes were green and flickering. And as she stood beside him, it seemed he already knew what she wanted to say.

Seeing that his feet were bare, she kicked off her shoes and peeled off her socks, grinning as Casper did the same. Then she stretched out her wings and drew herself tight, feeling the pull of the invisible archer. Somewhere far behind, Magnolia heard the sound of laughter. She didn't look back to see where it came from. Instead, she lifted her chin to their secret sky.

"Ready?" said Reuben.

"Steady," said Casper.

"Go!" said Magnolia.

Chapter 9:

The Secret Language

Magnolia Moon is a very good dancer. It was the moon that taught her how, when it led her through the weeds and over the wall at 84 Crocus Cottage. She has a dance for every occasion: storms, Wednesdays, stripey socks – even roast potatoes.

Just like the moon, Magnolia is always spinning. Circling the town of Thistledown each day and night. Magnolia can do it with her eyes closed. But she never does, since she is far too curious to look away. Unless, of course, you *want* her to. Then,

Magnolia is very good at pretending to close her eyes.

"I would be a strawberry," said Magnolia, still dizzy from spinning with Imogen May.

"Why?" said Imogen May, stretching her jelly snake until it snapped.

"Because strawberries are always going to nice places: picnics, parties, weddings. You only find them at the very best things."

"I once found a strawberry in Felix's nappy. He was saving it for later."

"Oh," said Magnolia. "That's not a nice place at all."

Magnolia knew all about nappies. She was an expert at changing Finnegan's. He could sit up and inch his way backwards now, and he liked to do it just as she was about to put his trousers back on. Sometimes she only managed to get one leg back in and would leave it like that until she got in trouble. Tonight they would be sharing their room for the first time. Magnolia was excited. Finnegan had been sleeping in a cot beside her parents' bed for the last six months, but Mama Moon said he was ready to come and sleep in her room now. Not that Finnegan slept much at all. Her parents were always up at night. The staircase was grouchier than ever. Even Atlas was out of sorts.

"Banana, then."

"That's against the rules," said Imogen May.

"Why?"

"Because technically a banana is a fruit *and* a herb. If we're allowed to pick herbs too, then I wouldn't have chosen a kiwifruit and would have picked basil so that everybody would like me."

"OK, well, let's say you *can* pick a fruit or a herb, but only if the herb is named after a fruit, like pineapple sage."

"So bananas don't count then?"

"I guess not," said Magnolia, feeling dizzier still. "Then I choose lemon thyme."

Imogen May rolled her eyes.

"You are such a show-off."

Magnolia heard a car pull into the driveway. Imogen May's dad had come to pick her up.

"By the way," said Magnolia softly as they walked to the gate. "Everybody *does* like you."

"Everybody except Madeline Phipps," said Imogen May.

Madeline Phipps was a popular girl at Imogen May's new school. She whispered and laughed every time Imogen May walked into a room or put up her hand.

"Don't worry about Madeline Phipps," said Magnolia. "She probably has a scorpion bite on her bottom that's very itchy." Which was what Grandma Moon said about bullies. "That's why she's so mean and scratchy all the time."

Imogen May chewed her bottom lip.

"Besides," said Magnolia, sheepishly. "*I* like you. Very much."

Imogen May beamed.

"You're bananas," said Imogen May.

Magnolia shook her head.

"*Lemon thyme*. Actually."

Almost as soon as Imogen May had gone, Magnolia heard a knock at the door.

It was Casper Sloan with his dog, Bonnie. Bonnie was a Basset Hound who loved porridge. Her ears were so long that they had to be tied up with an old pair of tights when she ate her breakfast to stop her dragging golden syrup through the house.

"Hi, Casper."

"Da! Da!" called Finnegan from his high chair.

"Hey Magnolia, we were wondering if you had a spare pumpkin? We're making pumpkin soup for dinner, but we don't have any ... *pumpkin.*"

"Come and choose one," said Magnolia. "We have a bumper crop!"

Casper smiled and proceeded to make a series of strange clicking sounds.

"What does that mean?" said Magnolia.

"It means 'thank you' in Owl."

Impressed, Magnolia led Casper and Bonnie to the veggie patch.

"Da! Da!" squealed Finnegan, squirming to get free.

"Jeremy!" called Mama Moon. "Can you come into the kitchen, please? Finnegan is calling for you again."

"Coming, my boy," called Daddy Moon. "Dada's here."

After dinner, Magnolia helped get Finnegan's bath things. She brought the tub and the washcloth from the bathroom. She put the bath on the kitchen table and filled it up with saucepans of warm water. Then she dipped her elbow in to check the temperature.

When Mama Moon lowered Finnegan into the sudsy water, he kicked his legs and sucked on the soapy washer.

"Yuck!" said Magnolia, trying to prise the washcloth out of his mouth. Finnegan would not surrender it.

"You did the same," said Mama Moon. "Drank plenty of bathwater in your time."

"There's probably *wee* in there."

"Probably," agreed Mama Moon.

When Finnegan was dressed in his vest and stripey jumpsuit, Magnolia put down the side of his cot. Their room was ready.

"Do you like our new curtains?" she said, pointing to the yellow daisies. "I chose them."

Finnegan did like the curtains. He also liked

Magnolia's books. He stuck his arm through the bars of his cot, reached across to her bookshelf and pulled one out.

"Finnegan, no!" she cried as he chewed on the corner of her book of Greek myths. "That's mine!"

But it was too late. The corner was already dented and covered with slime.

Magnolia reached in and ripped the book away from him. Finnegan screamed. Atlas jumped off Magnolia's bed and stalked out of the room. Magnolia inspected her book closely. Pegasus on the front cover was all right. Yet Orthrus, the two-headed dog on the back, was sticky with dribble.

"Here, take this," said Magnolia, passing Finnegan one of her old books about space.

But Finnegan didn't want that book. He wanted her special book.

"Da!" he wailed. "Da, da!"

"Coming, my heart," said her father. "Dada's here."

Daddy Moon picked Finnegan up and started doing bouncy squats along the hall.

"There, there, there," groaned the staircase sarcastically.

The squatting didn't seem to help. Finnegan still wailed, so Daddy Moon tried lunges instead.

Mama Moon stuck her head around the corner.

"He might need some more milk," she sighed, and both her parents disappeared again.

Magnolia tunnelled under the covers.

"Atlas," she called, poking her head out the end. "Here, boy."

Atlas did not come.

When Finnegan was quiet again, Mama Moon placed him down in his cot. Finnegan rolled over onto his knees and closed his eyes. Magnolia could just make out the tiny outline of his bottom in the air.

"Let's try it for a little bit," whispered Mama Moon. "If he keeps you up then we will have to think of something else. We can't have you going to school exhausted next week."

Mama turned off the light.

"I can't sleep without Atlas," Magnolia whispered.

"He'll come back when things have settled down."

Magnolia sighed and stared at the roof. She searched for the moon out the window. All the noise had scared it away too.

Magnolia woke. Finnegan was crying woefully. And not the woolly-bleaty-lamb-cry. The angry-screechy-cockatoo-cry. The house was dark except for a faint light coming from the lamp in the hall. She could hear her father snoring two doors down.

"Come on, then."

Magnolia picked Finnegan up and took him back to her bed.

His cheeks were hot and damp. She propped him up on a pillow and gave him her little finger to suck on. He pushed it away.

"Da," he said. "Da, Da!"

"Shh, Dada's sleeping," said Magnolia. "And you should be too. If you can't sleep in here then you will have to go back to your old room."

Then Finnegan started bobbing and wailing louder. He had seen the book. Her *special* book. Even though she had hidden it under a hat on her chest of drawers.

"Da!" he wailed. "Da! Daaaa!"

"Oh, all right, if you're very careful."

Magnolia reached across and got her book of Greek myths. Finnegan stopped crying immediately. He ran his hands over the back cover.

"Da!" he said triumphantly, slapping his hand on the picture of Orthrus.

"That's not Daddy," laughed Magnolia. "That's a dog."

"Da."

"Oh, *dog!*" said Magnolia. "You're saying dog? Is that a da?"

Finnegan blew some little bubbles and sat very still.

"Do you like dogs?" said Magnolia.

"Da," burbled Finnegan.

"I like dogs too. This is Orthrus, the two-headed da, and his brother Cerberus has *three* heads and a snake for a tail!"

Magnolia pulled her quilt up over them both. The moon was at the window, listening in. Even Atlas had returned and was in a tight ball at the end of the bed.

"Cerberus is a guard dog of the Underworld. I don't think they're very friendly dogs, though. Not like Bonnie. They eat people, not porridge. And they would never let you tie their ears up with tights."

Magnolia flicked through the book to find more pictures of the dog monsters. She read the entire chapter to Finnegan who helped by adding a few extra "da"s in the important parts.

When she had finished, Magnolia showed Finnegan how to make doggy shadow puppets on the wall, although she could only do a dog with one head. And when Finnegan was sick of that, she sang him the song about the little moon and tapped him on the bottom like her parents did until he went to sleep. Lifting him gently, she gave him a kiss and put him back into his cot. His tiny mouth twitched. She wondered if he was dreaming about dogs.

When Magnolia came downstairs, Finnegan was already in his high chair having breakfast and her father was playing the oboe.

Mama Moon was huffing and puffing like the Big Bad Wolf.

"He won't eat a thing," she said, waving a spoon in the air. "It must be his teeth. And he keeps calling out for your father, but he's ... *practising*."

Magnolia pulled up a chair, stifling a yawn.

"Did Finnegan keep you up last night?"

Finnegan looked at Magnolia. Magnolia looked at Finnegan.

"No," said Magnolia, holding in another yawn.

"If he keeps you up, we'll have to bring him back into our room."

"Da! Da!"

"I give up," said Mama Moon. "He won't take anything from me, he just wants you, Jeremy."

Magnolia got out her pencils. She started drawing a picture.

"What's that you're making?" said Daddy Moon, coming into the kitchen.

"It's a picture for Finnegan."

"Yikes!" he said, looking at the three-headed hound on the paper. "That's a little scary for a baby, don't you think?"

Magnolia gave it an extra head.

"Is that better?"

Daddy Moon grinned.

"Da!" said Finnegan. "Da! Da!"

"Don't be afraid," said Daddy Moon, "Dada's here."

Daddy Moon held a spoon up to Finnegan's lips, but Finnegan wrinkled his nose and turned away.

Then Magnolia gave him the picture.

Finnegan stared at the drawing.

Finnegan opened his mouth and took a big bite of scrambled eggs.

"See," said Mama Moon. "*Now* he wants to eat. He *is* happy you're here, Jeremy."

"Da," murmured Finnegan happily, smearing egg all over the picture.

Daddy Moon sat up straighter, looking as though he might pop with pride.

Magnolia smiled, watching on as Finnegan took another spoonful.

"He *is* very happy," said Magnolia and she didn't say anything more, since she didn't want to hurt her father's feelings, and they *were* both very happy that he was here. Besides, it was fun being the only person who could understand Finnegan's secret language.

"What are you going to do today?" asked Mama Moon.

"I thought I might invite Casper over," said Magnolia, "find him another pumpkin."

"Oh, yes?"

"And I thought," said Magnolia, glancing at Finnegan, "that I might invite Bonnie over, too."

"Good idea," said Mama Moon.

"Da!" clapped Finnegan.

Chapter Almost 10
The Secret Hero

The moon was wobbling.

Magnolia inched along the garden wall and stood beneath it.

"Don't worry!" she said, her arms spread wide, should it fall from the sky. "I will catch you!"

Inside, her mother was calling her name. Although Magnolia did not answer, as she was somebody else entirely. Last night, she was Arachne from her book of Greek myths; the weaver who was turned into a spider. She'd gathered up all the moon's silvery strands and woven a crown for a

tree. But tonight she was the hero, Perseus, flying with his pair of winged sandals – his gifts from the gods – rescuing those in need.

Except by now, it seemed that the moon did not need rescuing. That it was, in fact, Magnolia who was wobbling all along. So she sat on the garden wall and whispered it a secret instead.

The moon whispered back. It told her all sorts of things. About the oceans it moves, the stars that pass by. About what it's like to be old and full of holes. To live so far away. But there were some things it would not tell Magnolia: secrets it wanted to keep. Such as what she was getting for her birthday. And why her brother Finnegan crawls backwards and not forwards. And why it was taking so long to grow up. It wasn't easy being almost ten. And no matter how she prodded and poked for it to tell her, the moon only winked. So Magnolia flew away to find somebody else to rescue. And it wasn't long before she found someone.

"Don't worry," said Magnolia, waggling a sandal at her cat on the roof. "I will save you!"

But Atlas did not move, and for a moment she worried that he had turned to stone.

Then he blinked and twitched his whiskers, annoyed at having been disturbed.

And by the way he was glaring down at her, flicking his tail, Magnolia decided that he didn't need rescuing either. So she went inside to rescue her father from his book instead, as he seemed to be having a lot of trouble finishing it.

"What's it about?" said Magnolia.

"A hero, a rescue and a secret cave," said Daddy Moon.

Magnolia liked the sound of that.

"Is the hero almost ten?"

Daddy Moon shook his head and kept on reading.

Magnolia sighed. Nobody was ever almost ten in the adventures her parents read. Mama Moon said there was only one week to go before her birthday, but that was a lifetime if you were a rose in a vase, or a peach in a bowl.

"What happens in the end?" said Magnolia.

"I don't know," said Daddy Moon. "I haven't got there yet."

"Don't worry," said Magnolia, snatching the book and flipping to the last page. "I will tell you!"

"Don't!" said Daddy Moon, snatching it back.

"Don't you want to know?" said Magnolia.

"Of course I do."

"Then why don't you just read it now?"

"Because then it wouldn't be a surprise. And I would miss the middle bits."

Magnolia Moon didn't like the middle bits. They got in the way. She always went backwards so she could get to the end first: the end of the ice-cream cone, the end of the test, the end of the letter. Sometimes she even slept at the end of her bed to see if she could see the end of tomorrow from there, to find out what was going to happen.

"Magnolia!" called her mother. "Bed."

But since tonight Magnolia was not Magnolia, but rather Perseus, she decided to rescue one more person before she brushed her teeth. And judging by her scratchy voice and the large saucepan she was carrying to water the indoor pot plants, Mama Moon was just the person.

"Don't worry," said Magnolia, pulling the saucepan towards her. "I will save you!"

"Wait!" said her mother. "The handle, it's—"

Except it was too late.

The water sloshed all the way down the stairs.

"Oh!" moaned Mama Moon.

"No!" groaned the crotchety old wooden staircase as the water seeped into its cracks and grooves.

Then there was a wail from Magnolia's bedroom. She had woken Finnegan up.

"Sorry," said Magnolia, both socks slipping down with regret.

"That's OK," said Mama Moon.

Magnolia ran to get a towel and mopped up the

spill, scowling at the stairs, as messing about with a soggy towel wasn't exactly the adventure she had been hoping for.

"Mama," said Magnolia, wringing water into the saucepan. "How long does it take to grow up?"

"Not long," said Mama Moon.

"How many minutes?"

"Lots," said Mama Moon. "And barely any at all."

Magnolia sighed. Time was tricky like that. It could be long and short all at once. And it was always going backwards and forwards: getting stuck between yesterday and tomorrow. "When did you grow up?" asked Magnolia.

"Last Wednesday," said Mama Moon. "When I was fishing snails out of the letterbox."

Magnolia frowned. Those snails were always eating their letters. They even ate half of her invitation to Imogen May's tenth birthday party.

Back in her room, Magnolia put her pillow at the bottom of the bed and looked out the window. Finnegan was curled at the foot of his cot, sucking noisily on his thumb. She tried stretching her neck as far as it would go, but all she could see was the end of Atlas's tail. Then she turned to the wall, thinking of somebody else to be, since perhaps she wasn't a hero after all.

By breakfast the next morning, Magnolia had already fished three snails out of the letterbox, although she didn't *feel* any older. She was checking her reflection in a puddle when she heard huffing and puffing coming from the kitchen.

"What's wrong?" said Magnolia, running inside.

"It's Finnegan," said Daddy Moon. "I can't find him."

His eyes were wide and frightened.

"I put him on the floor just a moment ago and went to pick some snake beans," he said. "And when I came back he was gone. I've looked everywhere, but he's disappeared!"

Magnolia Moon knew all about strange disappearances. Vanishing gods and sucking whirlpools. She had read about them in her book of Greek myths. Although Finnegan Moon was not one for vanishing. Not when there were beans about. Finnegan *loved* beans.

Magnolia thought hard about where she would go if she were Finnegan, her springy hair coiling up in concentration.

Then her toes tingled. Her eyes glowed.

"Have you tried going backwards?"

Daddy Moon hadn't.

Crouching down on her hands and knees, Magnolia dropped to the place where Finnegan had started. Then she began crawling backwards. Under the kitchen table. Past the piano.

Behind the wilting old Christmas tree, still not taken down. Through cobwebs and a pile of odd socks. All the way to the wardrobe in the back corner until she couldn't go any further.

Then she heard a giggle. Magnolia stopped and looked in the shadowy depths beneath the wardrobe. And there was Finnegan. Imprisoned in a secret cave with no way of getting out. And it occurred to Magnolia that perhaps Finnegan was a lot like her. He didn't like the middle bits, either. He always went to the end first too: the end of his cot, the end of the bath, the end of the room.

"Don't worry," whispered Magnolia, reaching into the cave. "I will help you."

The gap was too small for her to squeeze under; her arms only just fitting.

She leaned in and tugged his soft round body, but Finnegan wouldn't budge.

"Try going forwards," said Magnolia. "Come on, you'll like it."

Finnegan only blinked at her.

"It's not as hard as it looks," said Magnolia. "You just put one knee out, then the other, and your hands will follow."

Magnolia went first and showed him how to do it.

And after a time, Finnegan followed. They inched forwards together, until Finnegan came unstuck.

"My hero!" said Daddy Moon, bouncing on his toes, as Magnolia rescued Finnegan.

Then he stood back to make room as the two of them crawled all the way through the kitchen and out the front door.

Inside, her mother was calling her name. And this time our hero did answer.

Since there was nobody else she would rather be.

"I'm here!" said Magnolia Moon.

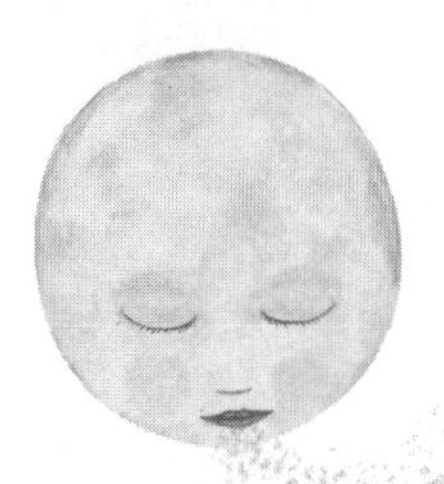